To Norah

May your wishes
come true —

Cub's Wish

Written by Angie Flores
Illustrated by Yidan Yuan

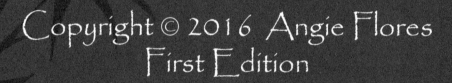

Cub's Wish

Dedicated to my husband and 3 cubs. May you never stop
dreaming, and making your wishes come true.

- Angie

Dedicated to my family and to all of my friends who encourage
me to keep pursuing my passion in art.

- Yidan

The stars sparkled especially bright as the
moon cast a blue shine over the bamboo forest.

Papa Panda and his Cub were out for a walk
to enjoy the night sky.

They found a nice hill on which to

sit and watch the stars.

A dazzling
twinkle caught
Cub's eye.

"Papa, why is
that star
brighter than
the rest?"

Papa smiled at the star's brilliance.
"Why, that's a wishing star, Cub. Go
ahead, make a wish. If the star feels your
wish is worth granting, then its magical
powers will make your wish come true."

Cub's eyes grew wide with excitement.

His tummy tickled at the thought the

star would grant him one wish.

But what would he wish for?

Papa watched Cub

in deep thought.

"Papa?" Cub asked.

"Should I wish to be a superhero? I could protect us from bad guys and help friends in trouble."

Papa chuckled. "You could, Cub, but you would not have much to protect. It's pretty quiet in the forest."

Cub thought about it. Papa was right. Things were pretty peaceful in the forest, and everyone got along.

"Papa? Should I wish
that I was very rich? I
could own all the bamboo
and be King of the forest!"

Papa smirked. "We have
more bamboo than we can
eat already. Having more
would be wasteful."

Cub knew Papa was
right. There was enough
bamboo for a hundred
thousand pandas and no
one would ever go hungry.

Wishing on a star was hard.

Cub wanted to

make sure that whatever

he wished for would be

granted.

So he gazed up at the star

and continued to think.

Out of the corner of his eye,

Cub could see his Papa

watch with a twinkle in his eye.

Cub perked up. "Papa, should I wish to be a robot with bright buttons and shiny lights? If I were a robot, I would never get tired, and I could stay up all night."

Cub started marching around like a robot. "Bee bop bee boop bing bing!"

Papa laughed and applauded Cub's performance. "Well, Cub, that sounds like it might be fun, but hugging a box of metal wouldn't be as nice as hugging your fur."

The moon rose higher as Cub

sat lost in ideas.

What else could he wish for?

Cub thought about his cozy

forest home filled with all the food

he needed.

He loved his warm cuddles from

his mama and papa and had lots of

friends to play with.

It seemed like he had everything

he could ever really ask for.

"Papa?" Cub asked. "What would you wish for?"

Papa looked into Cub's eyes and smiled.

"My wish would be to always feel as happy

as I do right now."

Cub thought that

was perfect.

"Papa?"

Cub asked.

"Can we share

that wish?"

Papa smiled and nodded.

Cub looked up to the sky,

focused on the wishing star

and said,

"I wish I could always be

as happy as I am

right now."

Cub nuzzled in and
hugged his papa
really tight.
Papa hugged back.
"See,"
Papa whispered,
"My Cub's wish
is coming true."

CPSIA information can be obtained
at www.ICGtesting.com
Printed in the USA
LVHW07*0331030318
568226LV00004BA/4/P